The
JESSAME
Stories

Other Titles by Julia Jarman

The Crow Haunting
The Ghost of Tantony Pig
Ghostwriter
Hangman
Ollie and the Bogle
Peace Weavers
Poppy and the Vicarage Ghost
The Time-Travelling Cat and the Egyptian Goddess
The Time-Travelling Cat and the Tudor Treasure
The Time-Travelling Cat and the Roman Eagle
When Poppy Ran Away

The JESSAME STORIES

JULIA JARMAN

Illustrated by Duncan Smith

Andersen Press • London

For Vanessa Aduke Olusanya, now Mrs
Pearce, who shared her childhood
memories with me. With love.

Published in Great Britain in 2005 by
Andersen Press Limited,
20 Vauxhall Bridge Road, London SW1V 2SA
www.andersenpress.co.uk

First published in Great Britain in 1994 by
Heinemann Young Books

Text copyright © Julia Jarman 1994
Illustrations copyright © Duncan Smith 1994

The rights of Julia Jarman and Duncan Smith to be identified as the author and
illustrator of this work have been asserted by them in accordance with the Copyright,
Designs and Patents Act, 1988

British Library Cataloguing in Publication Data available
ISBN 1 84270 454 0

Printed and bound in Great Britain by
Bookmarque Ltd., Croydon, Surrey

Contents

Contents

Jessame's Very Lucky Day

It didn't feel like a lucky day, not at breakfast time.

'Jessy, you're messy!'

Jessame – say "Jes-sam-mee" – didn't mind being called Jessy. She didn't mind being called Messy Jessy – or Affy – or Baddy Addy – or Olly – or Sanya – or even Lasagna. She was called all of them sometimes, because her full name was Jessame Aduke – say "A-doo-kay" – Olusanya. but she *did* mind being dabbed at rather fiercely with wet kitchen roll.

So she stiffened.

Her arms stiffened; her legs stiffened; the little plaits sticking out of her head stiffened. There was a red bow at the end of each plait, the exact red of her red and white dress, the red and white and *purple* dress now – because there were blobs of bilberry milkshake all down the front of it. Oh dear.

'Sorry, Mummy.'

Jessame could see herself and her mum in the mirror, two stiff people, one tall looking down, one small looking up.

Her mum had made the dress and matching ribbons — and the bilberry milkshake. Mrs Olusanya was very just-so and she liked Jessame to be just-so too. Jessame liked bilberry milkshake.

'Let's see, now.' Mrs Olusanya stopped dabbing and stood back — and her face went dimply. All the blobs had gone it seemed. She picked up Jessame's school bag and kissed her on her nose.

'All right. I suppose you couldn't help it, Messy Jessy. Here's your bag and here's Grandma. I must be off.'

And she was off, in a cloud of flowery perfume. Jessame could hear her high heels clitter-clattering down the stone stairs.

And Grandma, who was plump and comfortable, was standing in the doorway with Baby Mark in his buggy.

'Come on now, Jessame.'

But now Jessame could feel cold wet

patches soaking through to her vest. Grandma saw them. She got dry kitchen paper and dabbed – gently.

'Don't worry, Jess, they'll soon be dry. Look out there. The sun's smiling on Holly Gardens this morning.'

Jessame Aduke Olusanya lived in Holly Gardens, at 56 Holly Bush House. She lived with her mum, her baby brother, and Grandma and Grandpa Williams. Holly Bush House was a block of flats and number 56 was a specially nice one on the second floor. It had a very smart green front door and a very smart green verandah. The green verandah stretched from number 58 to number 52, and on summer evenings all the neighbours came out and sat on the green verandah, and they talked – but more about the neighbours later.

On this particular Monday morning a nearly dry Jessame was hurrying down the stairs two at a time to get to the bottom first. And Grandma Williams was a bit behind her, bumping Mark's buggy down the stairs with just the right amount of bump, so he was gurgling and shrieking. And then Jessame was opening the door at the bottom, and Grandma and Mark were gliding through majestically. Well,

Grandma was gliding majestically, because she was pretending to be The Queen — and Jessame was pretending to be a royal doorman. Grandma and Jessame liked pretending.

But suddenly the royal doorman closed the door with a bang — and she *ran*, for Jessame was Jessame again and the best bit was over. The next bit wasn't so good. Now, Jessame wanted to take hold of Grandma's hand and keep hold, because they were coming to the Railway Arches — and they were a little bit scary.

In fact they were a big bit scary. They were tall and dark and they blotted out the smiling sun and they *rumbled*. Jessame didn't like them at all. She felt very silly not liking the arches, so she hadn't told anyone, not even Grandpa. She knew that the rumbling was really the trains on the railway overhead. She had watched the trains go by from the window of Holly Bush House and from the green verandah, which was even nearer, but underneath the Railway Arches was dark and gloomy. There were sticking-out bits and hiding places and cobwebs like grey curtains, and, worst of all, she couldn't help thinking of the Big Bad Troll who lived under the bridge in the story about the Billy Goats Gruff.

So she tightened her grip on Grandma's

hand, because they were going under *now*. And any moment the rumbling might start, and the Big Bad Troll would jump out of the darkness and say, "I don't like you, Jessame Olusanya. *I'm going to eat you up!*"

She felt especially silly being frightened because she was a Big Sister now and Baby Mark who was only one, didn't seem even a little bit scared. Nor did Grandma.

So she tried to think of something to say to show she wasn't scared.

But she couldn't think of anything to say.

So she tried to hum a tune.

But she couldn't think of a tune to hum.

So she tried to walk very fast, hoping that Grandma would walk fast too — or even run — so they would be out of the tunnel before the rumbling came, but Grandma *stopped*.

She stopped right underneath the darkest, gloomiest, creepiest, cobwebbiest bit of the arch and she said, 'Do you know what's very lucky, Jessame?'

Jessame shook her head. Then she tried to pull Grandma as if she were in a hurry to get to school — because she *was* in a hurry to get to school. But Grandma asked her question again.

'Do you know something that's really

lucky, Jessame? So lucky that if this lucky thing happened right now, you would have good luck for all the rest of the day?'

Jessame shook her head again and her red bows rustled.

'Well, don't you want to know?'

Jessame nodded and said, 'Yes, Grandma Williams,' in a very small voice.

'Well now, it's this,' said Grandma, but then she paused, and seemed to be listening for something.

And Jessame listened for something and hoped she wouldn't hear it.

'Well,' said Grandma. 'If you're lucky enough to be walking under a bridge at the *very same time* that a train is going over the bridge you're sure to have a very lucky day.'

And then it happened. First a distant rumbling, then a closer roaring, then thunder overhead which made the walls shake and the railings rattle and little bits of cobweb come floating down like black snow. Then it was quiet again – and Grandma was walking very fast, pulling Jessame's hand.

'Come on. Let's see what the day will bring. Let's see if it's going to be your lucky day.'

And do you know what?

At school, Jessame got a gold star for jumping off the box with a straight back in gymnastics, and she had to show everyone else how to do it. Mrs Pearce said, 'Look at Jessame, everyone. Her body is a straight line. A straight line.'

Then Mrs Pearce picked her to give out the coloured pencils *and* take the register to the secretary – which meant going down three sets of stairs. And, to top it all, Jason the caretaker's son invited her to his party. Jessame had always wanted to see inside the caretaker's house, so she was very, very pleased.

She told all this to Grandma when she came to meet her from school, and on the way home Grandma stopped at the sweet shop and bought some Jubblies.

Jubblies were enormous pyramids of ice lolly, and they came in two flavours, orange and raspberry. Jessame's favourite was orange because, though the raspberry was a prettier colour, the orange one was fruitier and Grandma bought *two*. One was for Jessame to eat now and one was to eat later. Jubblies were so big that Jessame couldn't eat a whole one. She gave the last bit to Mark, and Grandma said she was very kind.

After supper she sat on the green verandah with Grandpa, watching the sky turn pink and soft-grey like pigeon feathers, and she shared the second Jubblie with him.

'And what sort of day have you had, Jessame Aduke?' Grandpa always called her Jessame Aduke.

'A Very Lucky Day, Grandpa, a Very Lucky Day indeed, thank you very much.'

And she told him about all the good things that had happened and the Big Bad Troll who didn't live beneath the Railway Arches. Then Mum and Grandma brought chairs onto the green verandah, and together they watched the soft-grey sky darken, till the moon appeared, a sliver of silver in a velvet sky.

'God bless the moonlight,' said Grandma as she always did.

'God bless the moonlight,' said Jessame.

Hiding from Uncle Sharp

'I'm on dry land, Dorinda.'

Grandma had made sausages and onion gravy for dinner.

Grandpa loved onion gravy. He loved all sorts of gravy. He liked his dinner to float in it. Today Grandma hadn't given him enough. But Grandpa didn't say, 'You haven't given me enough gravy, Dorinda.' Or, 'Please may I have some more gravy, Dorinda.' Dorinda was Grandma's first name.

He said, 'I'm on dry land, Dorinda. I'm on dry land.' And he dabbed at his face with a handkerchief as if he were stranded on a scorching desert island and needed water – or gravy – desperately.

And Grandma would say, 'Put that away, Thomas,' – referring to the handkerchief. Then she would give him some more gravy.

Grandpa was like that. You had to know him really well to understand him – and Jessame knew him very well indeed.

Grandpa had been a sailor and lots of his expressions were old sea sayings. So were Uncle Sharp's. Uncle Sharp was Grandpa's best friend. He was still a sailor. He lived at number 52 Holly Bush House, at the other end of the green verandah. But he wasn't there very often. Mostly he was away at sea. But when he came back, it was like Christmas and everybody's birthday all on the same day. Except that it was for more than one day. It was stories and presents for weeks at a time. Till he was gone again.

Jessame always hid when Uncle Sharp came round, and he came round a lot when he was at home. She didn't know why she hid or when she had started hiding. And she didn't know how she knew it was Uncle Sharp at the door. But she liked him a lot and she just *knew*. She would hear the knock at the door and she *knew*.

Then she would race to find a hiding place before her mum or Grandpa or Grandma opened the door. Mostly she hid under the table. It had a fringed tablecloth which nearly reached the floor. The tablecloth was red and the light shone through, making under-the-table into a cosy cave. From inside the cave Jessame would hear a voice say, 'Where's Jessame today? Where is my Little Flower?'

That was Uncle Sharp. Little Flower was his special name for her.

Uncle Sharp was her special name for him.

Grandpa always called him George.

Grandma always called him Mr Sharp.

Jessame always called him Uncle Sharp –

though he was big and bearish with no sharp edges at all.

Anyway, Uncle Sharp would say again. 'Where is my Little Flower?' And Grandpa would reply, 'I don't know, George. But I wish she would return. It isn't the same without Jessame.'

'It's not so conversational,' said Grandpa.

'It's not so ticklesome,' said Uncle Sharp.

'It's not so songsome,' said Grandpa, because Jessame always sang to him the songs she had learned at school.

And so they would go on, and if she was spying from a chink in the folds of the red cloth, she might see Uncle Sharp take out his pipe and start to fill it with baccy and she would smell the spicy smell and think — Isn't he going to? Isn't he going to? And then just as she thought he wasn't going to, he would put down his pipe and say, 'Hadn't we better look for her, Thomas? Hadn't we better cast about?'

And then they would both get up.

And they would both look in the cupboard.

Then they would both look behind the sofa.

They would look behind the curtains, and they would open the door to see if she was on the

21

green verandah, but they never, never, never looked in the place where she was.

And all the time this was going on, Jessame would be hugging her knees and silently shaking with laughter, and trying to stop the laughter spilling from her mouth.

Then, suddenly it would go dark under the table, and Grandpa and Uncle Sharp would be standing really close — shutting out the light from the lamp — and then Jessame would *jump out* with a yell of 'Here I am!' And there would be hugs and kisses and tickles and wriggles and hoistings high.

But one day something awful happened. It happened like this. Jessame found a new hiding place. It was in an old sea-chest. Jessame's mum kept materials in it. It had been Grandpa's. He said it had been a medicine chest long ago and had probably belonged to a ship's doctor.

The chest had lots of painted flags inside the lid, and Jessame knew the names of all the countries where the flags had come from, because Grandpa had told her. And he'd told her stories about all the different countries because he had been to them.

Anyway, on this particular awful day — it was a Saturday — Jessame had taken the materials out and put them in a cardboard box – because she'd planned a big surprise. It was Uncle Sharp's first day home after a long voyage to Africa. She knew he was home because his kitbag was on the verandah outside number 52. He must have come home in the middle of the night. The kit bag was Uncle Sharp's *AT HOME* sign – but no one had seen him yet. Jessame's plan was this: instead of hiding under the table when Uncle Sharp came, she would hide in the old sea-chest.

So when she heard the knock on the door which she knew was Uncle Sharp's knock, and while her mum and Grandpa and Grandma were all greeting him at the door and telling him to come in – which he couldn't do because they were all blocking the doorway – Jessame climbed into the chest. It was behind the living room door next to the small sofa.

As soon as she'd pulled down the lid, she wished she hadn't. It was dark inside and cramped, but she was *longing* to hear Uncle Sharp say, 'Where is Jessame? Where is my Little Flower?' So she stayed in the chest as quietly as she could, which wasn't very difficult, because her chest was pressed against her knees and it was almost impossible to move or speak.

And at last she did hear him say, 'Where is Jessame? Where is my Little Flower?'

And she heard Grandpa reply, 'I don't know George, but I hope she won't be long. It's not the same without Jessame.'

Then she heard another voice say, 'Where is Jessame? Where is my Little Flower?'

The other voice said it twice: 'Where is Jessame? Where is my Little Flower?'

And she heard Uncle Sharp say, 'I hope she'll like my special present, Thomas.'

'There's no saying, George, no saying. Jessame Aduke has a mind of her own. You know that. I do miss her, you know.'

And hidden in the chest, Jessame heard the familiar refrain.

'It's not so conversational without Jessame.'

'Not so ticklesome.'

'Not so songsome.'

And then, that other voice again:

'Where is Jessame? Where is my Little Flower? Where is Jessame? Where is my Little Flower?'

It was like Uncle Sharp's voice and yet *not* like it, and then there was Uncle Sharp's own voice. 'Quiet, Jacko. You'll let the cat out of the bag.'

Letting the cat out of the bag was one of Grandpa's expressions too. Jessame knew that it had nothing to do with cats. It meant – 'Quiet, Jacko, you'll give away a secret.' Now who was Jacko? And what was the secret?

Now Jessame was *desperate* for Uncle Sharp and Grandpa to start looking for her. It was really horrid and dark and cramped in the old sea-chest. But though she could hear the chink of cups and plates from the kitchen where Mum and Grandma were getting supper, she couldn't hear any sign of Uncle Sharp and Grandpa at all. She wished she was in her old hiding place under the table, where she could see and smell. Then she would know whether Uncle Sharp had taken out his baccy and was going to start filling his pipe. She would know if they had started to look for her.

Then, just as she was about to push up the lid because she couldn't stand it any longer, she heard the longed-for voices.

'Well, shall we cast about, George? Shall we look for Jessame Aduke?'

She heard their footsteps, and she imagined them looking in the cupboard and behind the sofa, looking behind the curtains and on the verandah. Then she knew they were standing in front of the table because it went very quiet – and she decided to jump out of the chest.

She pushed against the lid with her head – *but it didn't move.*

She pressed and pressed till it hurt her head and she even managed to push one hand against the lid, but it still didn't move. Then she cried out in what she hoped was a big loud voice, 'Help! Help! Let me out!' But her mouth wouldn't open wide because now the top of her head was pressed against the lid and her chin was pressed against her knees – so her voice came out small and squeaky.

And outside, Uncle Sharp and Grandpa were talking again.

'Asleep in the hold, do you think, George?'

'It's distinctly possible, Thomas. Let's look.'

Then she thought they must be looking under the table, and they were, because next she heard them say, 'She's not there. Little Flower isn't there!' And they sounded worried.

So she yelled again, or tried to yell, 'Help! Help! Let me out! LET ME OUT!'

'Did you hear what I heard, George?'

'Indeed I did, Thomas.'

Then Grandpa said, 'Tell us where you are,

27

Jessame Aduke.'

And Uncle Sharp said, 'Tell us where you are, Little Flower.'

And the other voice said, 'Where is Jessame? Where is my Little Flower? Where is Jessame? Where is my Little Flower?'

And Jessame said, 'I'm in the old sea-chest.'

It took them several minutes to get her out because the catch was stuck, but it wasn't so scary in the chest once Grandpa and Uncle Sharp knew where she was. She knew they would get her out. And they did.

Then there were hugs and kisses and hoistings in the air and they made her promise never to get in the old sea-chest again, or get in *anything* like that without asking a grown-up first. And while Jessame was sitting on Uncle Sharp's shoulders she found herself looking into the round eye of a parrot. So that's who Jacko was! He was grey with white cheeks and a red tail and he was perched on the top of the bookshelf. He liked books, Uncle Sharp said. Uncle Sharp had brought him all the way from Sierra Leone in Africa, but he hadn't been *packed* in a crate like some poor parrots Jessame had seen on the television. He had lived in Uncle Sharp's hotel room in Freetown, and then in Uncle Sharp's

cabin for the long, long voyage and Uncle Sharp had taken him on deck sometimes, and taught him to speak.

'Hello, Jessame. Hello, Little Flower,' said Jacko.

'Hello, Jacko,' said Jessame. 'Can you say anything else?'

'One two four five,' said Jacko. He put out a claw and Jessame shook it. Then she told Uncle Sharp that Jacko was very beautiful and *quite* clever, and Uncle Sharp said he was very glad that Jessame liked him, because if they all liked him, Jacko could stay with the family.

And they did all like him, so Jacko stayed, though Grandma said she had her doubts.

Jessame and the Very Fancy Dress

There was a Very Fancy Dress in the museum opposite Holly Bush House. It was a beautiful blue dress with a very tiny waist and a very sticking-out skirt with *paniers*. Grandpa said they were paniers. They were like big bows and they made the sticking-out skirt look even more sticking-out, and they made the tiny waist look even tinier. Grandpa said the Very Fancy Dress looked very uncomfortable, but Jessame said it was beautiful. It was the most beautiful dress she had ever seen.

There were lots of beautiful dresses in the museum including a duchess's wedding dress with silver lace, but it wasn't as beautiful as the Very Fancy Dress. Besides, as Jessame told Grandpa, the duchess's dress shouldn't really have been there. It was a grown-up's dress and the museum was a museum of childhood, wasn't it? The Bethnal Green Museum of Childhood was its proper name, and Jessame liked to give things their proper names. The museum was full of things belonging to children in days gone by. It was full of games and toys and clothes – just a few clothes – which children played with and wore long ago, and Jessame loved it.

She loved it so much she called it *her* museum – and Grandpa said it *was* her museum because it was everybody's museum. It belonged to the people. That's why it was free. It really was free. You could go in as often as you liked *without paying* and look at all the lovely things. Jessame went ever so often. She could see it from her bedroom window and if the day was grey when she woke up, and if she didn't have to go to school, she would say, 'Let's go to my museum today, Grandpa Williams. Do you think that's a good idea?' And nearly always Grandpa would say, 'Yes, Jessame Aduke. That's a very good idea.'

Grandpa's friend, Mr Sanderson, was the doorman at the museum, and he always opened the door very grandly when he saw Jessame and Grandpa coming up the big circular drive. And he always looked very surprised when Jessame wouldn't go in! His mouth fell open and his eyebrows disappeared under his peaked cap — every time! Even though he knew that Jessame never went in straight away. She always carried on walking — or running sometimes — past the doorway and right round the other side of the big circular drive, and half way round again, till she reached the doorway again, and then she would go in.

And this time Grandpa would stand on one side of the entrance, and Mr Sanderson would stand on the other and Jessame would enter very grandly. Mr Sanderson would touch his peaked cap and say, 'What would Miss Olusanya like to see first today?' And Jessame would stop and say, 'The dolls' houses I think, and then the toy theatre with the button you press to change the scenery.' Or sometimes she would say, 'The motor cars and then the finger puppets, please.' She always kept the Very Fancy Dress till last.

And Mr Sanderson would say, 'I think you know the way, Madam, but if you need any assistance . . .'

But Jessame wouldn't be there. She didn't need any assistance.

She did know the way — straight ahead to the dolls' houses in their big glass cases, or up the stairs to the ride-on toys and the pretend shops, also in big glass cases. That was the only thing wrong with the museum, the big glass cases. How she longed to ride on the ride-ons or buy things from the pretend shops or play with all the tiny things inside the houses. She could never make up her mind which was her favourite house. She very much liked the one called Miss Miles's House because the notice said Miss Miles had made it *when a child, in the 1890's.* It was very grand. It had ten rooms filled with pretty furniture and on the floor of the parlour there was a tiny book, as if a small person had just stopped reading it and was coming back in a minute. Jessame wondered how old Miss Miles had been when she'd made her house, and whether she'd made all the things to go in it.

Nuremberg House was very interesting too, and the most interesting thing in that was a baby walker! It was just like the one Baby Mark had, like a pair of pants in the middle of a square frame with wheels. Mark sat in his and walked at the same time. But this one was over three hundred years old. It had been made in 1673! Grandma had been ever so surprised when Jessame had told her. In fact Jessame had to take her to see it, because Grandma had thought baby-walkers were a modern invention. She'd said, 'Well I never,' three times over when she saw it and, 'Well now, there's nothing new under the sun is there?'

So Jessame always went to see the houses, and she nearly always went to see the magic lantern shows. There were lots of these, and when you pressed a button a picture lit up, and when you pressed the button again the picture changed. Jessame's favourite was of the zoo in Paris. One picture was of a lion in a cage, and when you pressed the button it jumped out of the cage! Then Jessame would run — not because she was frightened — but because she couldn't wait any longer. She ran up the stairs, round the balcony to the other side, to the glass cases with costumes — and there was the Very Fancy Dress.

Each time she saw it, it looked more beautiful and Jessame stood still and gazed at it. She pressed her nose against the glass and imagined herself as Cinderella going to the ball. She imagined herself riding in a carriage and dancing with the prince. Sometimes she imagined so hard that she wouldn't notice Grandpa standing beside her, till he said, 'It's midnight, Cinderella. Time to go home before you turn into a pumpkin.' And for a moment she would believe him. Then she would sigh and say,

35

'Isn't it the fanciest dress you've ever seen, Grandpa Williams?' And Grandpa would chuckle.

But it *was* the fanciest dress she had ever seen, and it *was* her museum, so when one Friday at school Mrs Pearce said, 'We are going to have a Fancy Dress Party, children,' Jessica knew exactly what she would wear. Mrs Pearce went on to explain what she meant because some people didn't know what a Fancy Dress Party was. She said that it didn't mean just wearing your best clothes, your party clothes, it meant dressing up as somebody or something else. Jessame hardly listened. She didn't need to.

She told Grandma all about it as soon as they met at the school gate. 'And I shall wear the Very Fancy Dress from my museum,' she said.

And Grandma said, 'Don't set your heart on it, Jessame. I don't think you can borrow dresses from museums.' But Jessame said she thought she would be able to, just once.

She told Grandpa as soon as he got home from the telephone works and she told him that he must go to see Mr Sanderson the very next day and arrange to borrow the Very Fancy Dress, but even Grandpa shook his head. 'I think that's "Not Allowed", Jessame Aduke. You see, the dresses in the museum are very old and fragile.

If people started wearing them they might fall to pieces.'

Jessame said she wasn't people, she was just one person, and she made Grandpa promise that they would go the next day and ask Mr Sanderson. Grandpa said he would do better than that. He would ask the curator. She was the person in charge, but he still said he thought the answer would be "no".

When her mum came home, Jessame told her all about the Fancy Dress Party, and the Very Fancy Dress in the museum and how she wanted to wear it. Mrs Olusanya shook her head and said, 'Don't set your heart on it, Jessame,' – just like Grandma had, but she also said, 'I think I'll come with you tomorrow, Jessame. I'd like to see that Very Fancy Dress. We can all ask the curator.'

The curator said, no. She was very sorry but, no. It was just not possible. If she let Jessame borrow the dress, she would have to let everybody borrow the dress and she couldn't.

Jessame was upset. Everybody tried to cheer her up. Grandma said, 'Why not go as Mrs Tiggywinkle?'

Grandpa said, 'Why not go as a parrot? Jacko would like that.'

Jacko sat on Jessame's shoulder. He said, 'Like that. Like that,' and pecked her ear very gently.

But Jessame didn't want to go as anything else. She didn't want to go as a hedgehog or a parrot. She wanted to go as Cinderella in the Very Fancy Dress.

When she got to school on Monday the whole class were talking about their fancy dresses. They didn't sound a bit fancy to Jessame. Jason, the caretaker's son, was going as a beetle. His mum was making his costume out of dustbin bags. Jamila was going as a newspaper — wearing *newspapers*! The three McFiggins's were going as turtles. Jessame didn't want to be a beetle or a newspaper or a turtle. She wanted to be Cinderella in the Very Fancy Dress.

When her mum came to kiss her goodnight, Jessame told her how sad she was. Mrs Olusanya said, 'I'm sure you'll think of something else, Jessame.' But Jessame said she wouldn't. There was only one fancy dress in her head, and while it was there, there wasn't room for anything else. So then her mum said, 'Well let me think of something, Jessame. It will be a surprise. Just one thing, you must promise to try to like it a little bit. I don't want to try hard for nothing.'

So Jessame promised, and hoped she would be able to *look* as if she liked whatever her mum decided on. She didn't want to hurt her mum's feelings.

The funny thing was, that soon after that, she did start to be a little bit interested. Two nights later when she lay in bed listening to her mum's sewing machine whirring, she started to become curious, curious enough to get out of bed and get a drink of water, but when she got to the sitting-room door — and you had to go through the sitting-room to get to the kitchen — the door wouldn't open, and the whirring stopped.

'What is it, Jessame?' said her mum, who must have seen the door handle moving.

'I want a drink of water, please,' said Jessame.

'Well, get it from the bathroom,' said her mum.

'There isn't a cup in the bathroom,' said Jessame, who didn't know whether there was or not.

'Well, go back to bed and someone will bring you one.'

The someone was Grandpa.

'What's Mum making?' asked Jessame.

Grandpa tapped the side of his nose. 'It's a secret,' he said. 'Now go to sleep.'

The whirring began again. And it whirred again the next night. Jessame asked for a drink of water again and Grandpa brought her one.

'What *is* Mum making?' asked Jessame.

Grandpa tapped the side of his nose again.

'Please, Grandpa, give me a clue?'

Grandpa thought for a bit. Then he said,
> 'It's made by a worm
> But it won't make you squirm.
> It's made by your mum
> It will cover your tum

It's made by night
To give Jessame delight.'

Then he kissed her and put out the light.

Jessame lay in the darkness thinking. "Made by a worm" was a bit worrying. All she could think of were the whirly worm casts on the grass in Victoria Park. She didn't want to wear something which looked like mud; that *would* make her squirm. What could it be?

The whirring went on, night after night, but at last the day of the Fancy Dress Party arrived. Surely now, her mum would let her see? But no, at breakfast Mum said it wasn't quite ready yet. She would bring it to school in the afternoon.

'But what about your work?' said Jessame. 'What about Mr Hankins at the Post Office? Who will write his letters?'

Mrs Olusanya said that as it was a very special day, Mr Hankins had said she could have a day's holiday, to finish the dress and take it to Jessame and see the Fancy Dress Parade.

Everyone else took their fancy dress costumes in the morning. Mrs Pearce said they were to put them in the cloakroom till after lunch, but she had to say it three times before

42

everyone believed her. Jason said he ought to keep an eye on his beetle costume or it might scurry away into a dark corner and never be seen again. Jamila said someone might pick up her newspaper costume and take it away and read it, and the three McFiggins's said their turtles might jump into the lavatories and swim into the sewers if they were left alone.

Mrs Pearce said everybody was being very silly — which Jessame thought was a bit unfair, because she wasn't being silly at all. Then Mrs Pearce said if everyone wasn't very sensible, there wouldn't be a Fancy Dress Party — and then there was a scramble for the cloakroom. Morning lessons followed but they went very, very slowly.

Jessame kept looking at the door, but Mrs Olusanya didn't come. She hadn't come by dinner time, and Jessame could hardly eat for worrying whether she would come, and wondering what her costume would be like when she did. Mrs Lal, the dinner-lady, said she must eat a little bit more or she would be poorly in the afternoon, so there was Jessame in the dinner hall, trying to eat cornflake crunch, and looking at the door. At last she saw her mum. She was holding a very big suitcase. But it wasn't till they were in the classroom that her mum opened the case — and there was the Very Fancy Dress.

Jessame couldn't say anything. She just hugged her mum very tightly round the middle. The dress looked exactly like the one in the museum, except that the blue material was an even prettier blue and it had a silver haze. It had the same nipped-in waist that ended in two points, the same little covered buttons, the same lace round the top of the bodice and the ruffles round the cuffs, and of course the same sticking-out skirt with *paniers*. And there was something else which looked a bit peculiar, a bit like a cage with sausage-shaped things on it.

Mum said it was a frame to make the sticking-out skirt stick out more. She helped Jessame to put it on, and then to put the Very Fancy Dress over it. There was hardly room to stand. Mum and Jessame had to move two tables, which was quite difficult because there were so many children standing there, gazing at the Very Fancy Dress. And then there were Grandma and Grandpa! Grandpa had his camera.

'Look like a lady, Jessame Aduke!'
Click!
'Curtsey, Jessame Aduke!'
Click!

44

Then Jessame showed Grandma and Grandpa the silver haze in the blue material and the ruffles round the cuffs and the ever so tiny waist, and she said, 'Why did you say it was made by worms, Grandpa?'

'Because it's made of silk, real silk, made by silk worms.'

That was amazing. Grandpa said they could read all about it later. Right now he wanted to know if the Very Fancy Dress was very uncomfortable.

'No,' said Jessame, and she showed him the cage thing with the sausage shapes.

Grandpa thought they were very funny.

'They're to make your bottom stick out,' he said, 'and roll from side to side like a ship at sea. And do you know what they're called, Jessame Aduke? Do you know what their proper name is?'

'No.'

'Bum rolls,' said Grandpa.

'Quiet, Thomas,' said Grandma Williams, looking all around to make sure no one had heard him. Then she gave Grandpa a very hard stare and Jessame couldn't stop laughing.

Grandpa and the Magic Water

Jessame couldn't wait to see the photographs Grandpa had taken. He had taken lots of her at the Fancy Dress Party. He had photographed her parading in the Very Fancy Dress Parade, with Jason the Beetle on one side and Jamila as a newspaper on the other. He had taken her dancing in the Very Fancy Dress doing a dance called the Lambeth Walk, which Mrs Pearce had taught them, and he had taken her being the dog in The Farmer's in his Den. They had played lots of ring-games, including Pass the Parcel. Jessame thought Grandpa must have taken hundreds of photographs because whenever she looked at him, he seemed to be looking at her — and clicking. Other mums and dads took photographs too and so did Mrs Pearce.

When they were back in the classroom, getting out of their fancy dress clothes and into their ordinary clothes, Mrs Pearce said she would bring her photographs in next Friday. She was sending them away to be developed, she said. Jessame wanted to ask what "be developed" meant, but Jason was saying he would bring his photographs in sooner than that. He would bring his in on Wednesday, because his dad was taking his film to be developed at the chemist's in Bethnal Green Road. Then Gemma said she would bring hers in even sooner than that – probably on Monday – because her mum was taking her film to Boots the Chemists who did them very quickly if you paid extra, and her mum would pay extra.

It was Thursday. Even Monday seemed a long way off – four whole days. Jessame wondered where Grandpa would take their film to be developed. She hoped it would be a place where they did them quickly. On the way home she asked him. It was just Grandpa taking her home because Mum and Grandma had already gone to fetch Mark from the nursery school in Sugar Loaf Lane.

So Jessame said, 'Where are we taking our photographs to be developed, Grandpa?' and he said, 'We're not.'

Jessame was so shocked she forgot to ask

him what "be developed" meant. She just wailed, 'What do you mean *"We're not"*?' And Grandpa laughed.

'Sorry, Jessame Aduke. Don't look so woebegone. I don't mean we're not getting them developed. I mean we're not taking them to a shop or a chemist's.'

'Why not?'

'Because we're going to develop ours at home.'

Then Grandpa said something even more exciting. He said that Jessame would be able to see what "be developed" meant — if she wanted to — because *she* could help him develop the film. Jessame could hardly believe it.

'When?' she asked.

'We can start in the bathroom as soon as we get home,' said Grandpa. 'But to finish the job we'll have to wait till after supper when it's dark.'

It had to be very, very dark he said, and after supper they would turn the kitchen into a dark-room.

When they got home, Grandpa went to the cupboard in the kitchen and got out a box. Then he said, 'Get hold of the camera, Jessame Aduke, and follow me.'

Jessame followed Grandpa into the bathroom where he put the box on the bathroom floor. Then he took out a brown bottle.

'What's that?' asked Jessame.

'The Magic Water,' said Grandpa.

'The Magic Water!' Jessame gasped. Had she heard right?

She had. Grandpa said it again, 'The Magic Water.' He held up the bottle. Then he took two more bottles out of the box and put all three of them into the sink. Then he turned on the hot tap.

'We have to warm them up a bit,' he said. 'Please turn the tap off when the sink is full.'

Now Grandpa delved into the box again, and this time he brought out a round black container and a strange black bag – with sleeves. Then he brought out a thermometer, a pair of scissors and a measuring jar.

'I hope you're good at measuring,' said Grandpa.

Jessame said she was. She did lots of measuring at school.

'That's all right then,' said Grandpa. 'But first of all please take the lid off that container,' (It was called the tank, he said) 'and give me whatever you find inside.'

Jessame found what looked like a big white cotton reel.

'You do remember me putting the film in the camera, don't you, Jessame Aduke?'

Jessame did. She remembered buying the little canister and watching Grandpa open the camera and put it inside. He'd said it was full of brown plastic film. And she'd said, 'How does it become a photograph?' And he'd said it was all a matter of *light*.

Now it seemed it was all a matter of *dark*.

Dark – that's what the black bag with arms was for.

It was as dark as Marmite in there, Grandpa said, and that's where he would get the film out of the little canister and put it onto the white reel.

'But you can't get in there, Grandpa. It's not big enough.'

Grandpa laughed. 'Not me, Jessie Aduke, *my arms*. Look.'

Then, with the canister of film in one hand, and the tank and reel in the other, Grandpa plunged his hands into the sleeves of the black bag, and closed his eyes – to see better, *with his fingers*! he said.

Jessame thought that was very funny – almost as funny as the bulges Grandpa's wiggling fingers were making. She said it looked as if he had a cat in the bag!

But a few minutes later his hands came out again, and he handed Jessame the empty canister.

'Where are the photographs?'

'In there.' Grandpa pointed to the tank in his other hand.

'Can't we see them?' said Jessame.

'Not yet,' said Grandpa. 'You've forgotten something haven't you?'

He held something above his head.

'Abracadabra!'

'Oh! The Magic Water!' said Jessame.

'Right,' said Grandpa, 'and first you must take its temperature.'

He gave her a thermometer rather like the one Mum used to take Jessame's temperature with when she was poorly. Jessame dipped it in the Magic Water.

'Twenty Centigrade,' she said.

'Twenty Centigrade!' said Grandpa. 'Exactly! Bravo! And we need exactly 290 millilitres of it.'

Jessame measured 290 millilitres exactly in a measuring jar. Then she poured it onto the film through the special opening in the lid of the tank. Then she put on another lid and Grandpa picked up his stop watch. He said it took exactly one minute for the magic to start working. Jessame must hold the tank for exactly one minute and then she must tip it up. She could hardly wait.

She held the tank in both hands, then together she and Grandpa watched the second hand go round. She would never have thought a single minute could take so long. Sixty seconds! How slowly the hand went round the dial.

But at last it was nearly at the top and Grandpa started to count down.

'5 . . . 4 . . . 3 . . . 2 . . . 1! Tip it up, Jessame!'

And Jessame did.

'Now for the photographs! They must be ready now.'

But Grandpa said the magic had only just started. She must wait another whole minute and tip it up again!

And then again!

And then pour the Magic Water back into the bottle.

'Can we see the photographs now?' Surely Grandpa must say "yes".

But – 'No,' said Grandpa. 'We have to stop

the magic first. I told you it would take us all evening, Jessame Aduke.'

'How? How do we stop the magic?'

'With Stop Magic of course.' It was in the second bottle.

Now Jessame had to pour Stop Magic into the tank and shake it ever so hard. And then she had to pour away the Stop Magic and put Fix Magic in the tank. It was in the third bottle. She had to shake the Fix Magic for 30 seconds and let it stand for 60 seconds. Once again they had to watch the second hand creep round Grandpa's watch.

'Now!' she shouted as it reached the top, for the photographs must be ready.

'We've been doing this for *hours*,' she said.

'Fifteen minutes to be precise,' said Grandpa. 'But this is new magic you see, scientific magic. It takes a little longer than the old kind.'

It certainly did. Now Grandpa was saying they must wash the photographs.

'Wash them? Before we even see them. How?'

'The same way we did everything else.'

Grandpa got a jug of water and poured it into the tank. Then he poured it out again. He did this *five* times and Jessame did it five times and she thought she would burst with all the waiting. But at last Grandpa said, 'Just a few seconds more, Jessame Aduke. Then you can hang your photographs out to dry.' He handed her some tiny clothes pegs. Then with a cry of,

'Open Sesame!
Photographs for Jessame!'

he took the lid off the tank and handed her a long strip of pictures and she could see lots and lots of tiny photographs of herself. Magic!

Except that she thought she looked a bit odd.

Nevertheless she pegged them onto the little washing line which Grandpa had put up in the airing cupboard.

Grandpa looked at the photographs and seemed very pleased.

Jessame looked at the photographs and was very worried.

She *did* look odd. The magic had gone wrong. She had a white face and white hair and she looked very peculiar. All the blacks and whites were the wrong way round. Jason was a white beetle. Oh dear. She couldn't possibly show anybody these photographs.

She wondered what to say. Grandpa seemed so pleased. Hadn't he noticed? He was looking at her now.

'You do know that we're not finished yet, Jessame Aduke?'

'Oh?'

'These are only the *negatives*, you know, and in the negatives all the lights and darks are the wrong way round.'

Whoosh! She could breathe again!

'How do we make them the right way round?'

'We have to print them on special paper and we'll do that after supper. We must wait for the negatives to dry first.'

Just at that moment Grandma called them for supper. It was pepper pot, one of Jessame's favourites, but it was hard to eat and hard to stop asking questions.

'How long will the printing take?'

'About an hour,' said Grandpa.

'And will my photographs be ready tonight?'

'Yes, Jessame Aduke.'

'Really, Grandpa?'

'Yes, Jessame Aduke.'

It was *tingliciously* exciting. She would have her photographs before Jason, before Gemma, before everyone — and she had developed them herself!

Grandpa reminded Grandma that he and Jessame would need the kitchen after supper. Grandma said she must wash the dishes first, but she would make haste. Jessame helped clear the table and she helped wash the dishes. Then she made a notice saying DO NOT ENTER which she hung on the kitchen door. Grandpa asked her to. He said that no one must come in. Even a tiny little chink of light could ruin everything.

But at last Mark was in bed. Mum and Grandma were settled in the sitting room and Jessame went into the kitchen. And there was Grandpa sticking black plastic to the window with black sticky tape. Suddenly it went dark. He had switched off the light too, and it was very mysterious with just a slit of light sneaking in through the door-crack, but Grandpa soon put a stop to that with more sticky tape. Then it was utterly, utterly dark.

Jessame was just wondering how she and Grandpa were going to see enough to do anything, when a red light came on in the corner. Grandpa said it was a special light which didn't ruin things. It glowed like a hot coal. Now the kitchen felt like Merlin's cave. Anything could happen here!

'Jessame Aduke.'

Jessame jumped.

Grandpa was handing her some scissors. He had fetched the negatives from the airing cupboard – they were hanging over the sink now – but they needed cutting up, he said.

So Jessame cut the negatives into strips and Grandpa got the special paper out of a box. Then he said the printing could begin. He said Jessame had to press the negatives onto the special paper and cover them with a sheet of glass – to stop them from curling. Very, very carefully she did both these things – and then Grandpa *switched on the light*! 'GRANDPA! WHAT ARE YOU DOING?' Jessame screamed. 'Even a chink of light can ruin everything! You said so!'

But Grandpa laughed and said, 'Calm down, Jessame Aduke. We need 30 seconds of light here. Look.' He had his stop watch in his hand, and after 30 seconds he switched the light off again.

Then out of the darkness came a sound like a trumpet. 'Taran ta ta taa!' It was Grandpa, of course, announcing that the Really Special Magic was about to begin. It was time for the Magic Water again.

'Again?'

'Again.'

He had put three trays on the draining board. There was Magic Water in the first tray, Stop Magic in the second tray and Fix Magic in the third.

Grandpa said Jessame must choose a print and put it in the first tray. She chose the one with herself in the Very Fancy Dress standing between Jason the beetle and Jamila the newspaper in the Fancy Dress Parade. She put it into the Magic Water – and *nothing happened*!

Oh dear! Slow magic was bad enough. No magic was awful!

'Patience, Jessame Aduke.' Grandpa was behind her and his big hand covered hers. 'Wait one minute.'

So Jessame waited for nearly a whole minute and at last the Really Special Magic started to happen. It made Jessame tingle to look into the Magic Water and see first a shimmery round shape, and then her own dark, smiling face floating towards her! Then Jamila's, then Jason's — and the rest of their bodies. Jason was a shiny black beetle and Jessame in the Very Fancy Dress looked *beautiful*. The magic had worked perfectly.

Jessame's Very Bad Day

'Only three can play in the Play House.' Jessame stretched her arms across the doorway – to stop Tony Lumsley. Jamila and Gemma were inside. They had only just started playing, but Tony said he had got there first. He hadn't. It was a fib.

'Mrs Pearce said so,' said Jessame. 'Only three are allowed in.'

'Mrs Pearce isn't here,' said Tony. He was a big boy with a loud voice. 'So get out of the way.' He tried to push past.

'Don't do that,' said Jessame.

But Tony thought he was right and Jessame thought she was. Mrs Pearce had made the rule about only three in the Play House because there wasn't room for any more, and Mrs Pearce was away. Mrs Fell was in charge today. It was Friday afternoon.

'I'm coming in,' said Tony. And he pushed Jessame really hard. She crashed into Jamila, and Jamila crashed into Gemma.

'Mrs Fell! Look at Tony!' But Mrs Fell didn't hear Gemma calling her.

It was very noisy in the classroom and Mrs Fell was shouting at the three McFiggins's who were under the table. They said they were hiding from aliens.

'See, she doesn't mind,' said Tony, and he poked Jessame with the skipping rope he was holding. It hurt. Jessame was cross.

'You're not allowed and nor is your skipping rope!' she shouted.

That was true too. Skipping ropes were not allowed in the Play House. So Jessame grabbed it and threw it out. She hoped Tony would go and look for it but . . .

'OU . . .CH!'

There was a yell, then a silence, then a moan.

Looking out of the Play House, Jessame saw Mrs Fell rubbing the back of her head. Then she saw Mrs Fell picking up the skipping rope.

'Who threw this?' Mrs Fell sounded very cross.

Jessame kept very quiet.

'*Who* threw this?' said Mrs Fell again.

'*WHO THREW THIS?*' she shouted.

'Jessame did,' said Tony Lumsley.

Mrs Fell made Jessame stand by the blackboard for the rest of the afternoon, and she wouldn't let her have any milk at playtime. Jessame always had milk at playtime. Her mum paid for it, but Mrs Fell said Jessame must learn her lesson. She wouldn't let Jessame explain about the skipping rope. She wouldn't let anyone else explain. Jamila and Gemma wanted to, but she wouldn't let anyone talk at all. She made everyone sit down and face the front and copy from the blackboard – all except Jessame. She made Jessame stand so close to the blackboard that she couldn't see the writing and she wouldn't let her do anything.

So Jessame just stood there with her legs aching, longing for the bell to go. She was longing for Grandma to meet her. She was longing to tell her everything. Grandma would be *so* cross with Mrs Fell. Jessame knew she would, as soon as she knew what had *really* happened. Grandma would understand that it had been an accident. Grandma would explain to Mrs Fell. Mrs Fell hadn't even let her say she was sorry. Now Jessame wasn't sorry.

65

'I do not like you, Mrs Fell
Exactly why I *CAN* tell.'

She said this over and over again, silently, to keep her spirits up and stop her eyes prickling. What a horrid teacher. She hoped Mrs Pearce would be back tomorrow. Mrs Pearce was kind. What time was it? She couldn't see the classroom clock because it was behind her on the back wall, but it seemed ages before the bell went and then Mrs Fell kept Jessame in till last.

She said she hoped Jessame had learnt her lesson. Jessame didn't say anything, but when Mrs Fell did let her go, she raced into the cloakroom to get her coat, and she raced into the playground to see Grandma – and Grandma wasn't there. The playground was empty. All the other mums and dads and minders had gone. Jessame felt dreadful. What had happened? Grandma was always there, with Mark. She was never late. Oh dear. She must be on her way at least.

Jessame ran to the gate and looked up and down the road, but Grandma wasn't there either. What should she do? A shout made her turn round. She hoped it was Grandma, but it was Mrs Fell striding across the playground towards her. She was wearing a grey coat and tying a scarf round her head.

'Child! Wait!'

Jessame wanted to run, but her feet felt as if they were stuck to the playground. Then Mrs Fell was standing beside her with her hand held out. 'Hold my hand, child. I'm taking you home.'

It was horrid holding her hand, like holding a piece of raw fish.

Mrs Fell said Grandma had rung to say she'd been "voidably tained". That's what it sounded like. Jessame was wondering what "voidably tained" was when Mrs Fell started to walk very fast. She didn't stop walking till they reached the zebra crossing in Old Ford Road. Then she said, 'Don't think I'm looking forward to telling your family how naughty you have been, child.'

But she was, Jessame could tell.

She looked as if she was bursting to tell them.

So how could Jessame tell them the true story first? Mrs Fell was *steaming* along. She really was. Steam puffed out of her red face and her fish-hand was hot and steamy too.

They stopped again to cross Cambridge Heath Road. Jessame could see the Railway Arches now and she listened hard. She hoped and listened and listened and hoped that a train would be going over the Railway Arches just as she was walking under them. That would mean good luck — so far it had been a very unlucky day — but as they reached the Railway Arches there was no lucky rumbling sound. She tried to go slow but it was impossible. Mrs Fell was still steaming forward, gripping her hand hard now.

Then they were standing in front of Holly Bush House. 'Number 56 if I am not mistaken,' said Mrs Fell. She sounded as if she could never be mistaken.

She did slow down a bit as they climbed the stairs, and by the time they were going up the third flight, she was panting like a dog.

When Grandma opened the door of number 56 she said, 'You poor, dear lady. You must come in and have a cup of tea. I've put the kettle on.'

She made Mrs Fell sit down in the sitting room.

Jessame went into the kitchen with Grandma and said, 'She's not a poor dear lady, she's a *monster*!'

And Grandma said, 'You keep your mouth shut when you're talking to me like that, Jessame.'

It was one of Grandma's expressions and it meant that she was very upset to hear Jessame talking about her teacher like that. Jessame was so upset that she rushed to her bedroom.

First she cried, because she had wanted to cry all afternoon. Then she listened as best she could to what was going on in the sitting room next door — and she heard what she'd been

dreading. 'Jessame has been a very naughty girl today, Mrs Williams. *She threw a skipping rope at me.*'

She made it sound as if Jessame had done it on purpose. Surely Grandma could not believe her?

She waited for Grandma to say it was impossible, and she did hear her say that she was very surprised, and that Mrs Pearce said she was a very well-mannered, helpful girl, and then she heard Grandma coming into the bedroom.

She sat down on Jessame's bed. Then she said, 'What *is* all this about, Jessame?' And Jessame told her. Then Grandma went back into the sitting room and Jessame heard her say, 'I think there has been a mistake, Mrs Fell.'

'Oh?' said Mrs Fell.

'Yes,' said Grandma. She was very kind to Mrs Fell. She didn't say, you stupid woman or anything like that. She just said, 'I think we'll let Jessame tell you what she told me, shall we?'

Then Grandma called Jessame into the room and asked her to tell Mrs Fell what had happened. So Jessame did and she even said, 'I'm sorry I hurt you, Mrs Fell.'

And Mrs Fell looked very hot and *wriggly*.

Jessame thought she was going to say sorry but she didn't. She stopped wriggling and her mouth *stretched* as if she was trying to smile.

Then she said, 'Why on earth didn't you tell me all that, Jessame?'

And Jessame said, 'Because you wouldn't let me.'

Then Mrs Fell's mouth opened wide and Grandma said, 'Drink your tea, Mrs Fell, it's getting cold.'

Mrs Fell drank her tea and Jessame thought she would go then, but she didn't. She started to talk. She was sitting in Grandpa's chair and she started to talk a lot. She talked about the weather and the traffic and schools today, which she didn't seem to like very much. She didn't seem to like anything very much. She talked and talked – and stayed and stayed.

Grandma listened. Jessame went into her bedroom, but she could still hear Mrs Fell talking. She was still talking when Grandpa came home, though she had slowed down by then.

Grandpa said he was very pleased to meet one of Jessame's teachers. Then he said, 'Where's Jessame Aduke?' and Jessame called out, 'Here, in my bedroom!'

When she told Grandpa everything, he said, 'It is dangerous to throw skipping ropes, Jessame Aduke. You should look where you're throwing.' But it was obvious he understood because he hugged her. Then they both went back into the sitting room — and Mrs Fell was still there.

Grandpa said, 'You and Jessame seem to have had a very bad day, Mrs Fell.'

And Mrs Fell said, 'Yes we have.'

'But all's well that ends well,' said Grandpa. 'We can all make mistakes.'

Mrs Fell sort of grunted.

Then Grandma said, 'Well I must make haste with the dinner now. I don't want any mistakes with that.'

And Grandpa said, 'Do you want a hand in the galley, Dorinda?' But Grandma said she thought she could manage.

Soon, delicious cooking smells were coming out of the kitchen, and Grandpa said, 'Is that chicken okra I can smell?'

Jessame went to see.

'Yes it is,' she said, when she got back, 'and Grandma says it will be ready in twenty minutes.'

'Chicken okra?' said Mrs Fell. 'What's that then?'

Now Jessame thought that if she told Mrs Fell how delicious chicken okra was, Mrs Fell might start to feel hungry and go home and cook her dinner. So she described how Grandma fried chopped-up chicken with okra and onions. She had to explain that okra was a sort of vegetable which came from Africa and that some people called them lady's fingers!

Then she described how Grandma added peppers and spices and her own special stock, and how all of these were cooked together on the top of the stove so that their flavours blended, and then how they ate it with lovely nutty rice.

'Mmmmm,' said Mrs Fell, and Jessame thought she would get up and go.

But she didn't. She said, 'Well, that *does* sound tasty.'

And she seemed to make herself even more comfortable in Grandpa's chair, which made Jessame feel even more uncomfortable.

She didn't want Mrs Fell in Grandpa's chair. She didn't want Mrs Fell in Holly Bush House. She was just about to say, 'What are you going to have for your dinner, Mrs Fell?' – which she thought was more polite than, 'Why don't you go home, Mrs Fell?' – when Grandma called out, 'Jessame, lay the table please!' and Mum arrived home with baby Mark. She'd had to take him to the doctor's.

Grandpa said, 'This is one of Jessame's teachers — Mrs Fell. She very kindly brought Jessame home from school today.'

And Mum said, 'How good of you. Are you staying to dinner, Mrs Fell?'

There was a silence then, in which Jessame gave her mum a very hard stare. Then they all heard Mrs Fell say, 'Well, as you're asking, I don't mind if I do.'

And Jessame wanted to say, 'But we're not asking! Go home!'

But Grandma was saying, 'Lay another place, please, Jessame. I've just been telling Mrs Fell what beautiful manners you have.'

And Grandpa said, 'Well yes, we all have good manners in this family, I hope.'

So Jessame went to the kitchen to get another knife and fork, and Grandma said she was sure Mrs Fell was a lonely woman with no lovely family to go home to.

Jessame didn't say anything.

Mrs Fell stayed for dinner and she stayed on after dinner. She talked and talked about all the things she didn't like — there were ever such a lot of them — and everybody listened politely.

Grandpa did say once, 'Goodness gracious me, is that the time? I think that clock needs winding.'

And Grandma said, 'It's nearly your bedtime, Jessame,' a full half an hour before she usually did.

When she went off to run the bath, Mum said she would fill Jessame's hot water bottle. She went into the kitchen and Grandad said, 'Jacko's bedtime too I think.' He got up to put Jacko's cover on, and then a most extraordinary thing happened.

Jacko, who hadn't said anything all the time that Mrs Fell had been there, said, 'What are you sitting there for?'

And Mrs Fell was the only person still sitting down!

He said it again, very clearly, 'What are you sitting there for?'

And Mrs Fell got up! Grandpa got her coat for her.

When she'd gone, Grandpa said, 'Clever old Jacko. Who taught him to say that, I wonder?'

'I wonder?' said Grandma. 'It's strange how he's never said that before.' Then she *tickled* Grandpa!

Aunt Gbee and the Birthday Surprise

Jessame wasn't sure about Aunt Gbee. She arrived one Tuesday morning in a taxi while Jessame was still in bed. Jessame heard a beep and rushed to her window and there she was in the street below, a tall lady in a long yellow dress with wavy lines on it. The wavy lines were blue and maroon — maroon was reddish purple — and Aunt Gbee wore a piece of the same material round her head. It made her look even taller. She was waving and shouting, and Mum and Grandma and Grandpa were waving and shouting too — from the green verandah. Then Mum was outside too, hugging and kissing Aunt Gbee. She had rushed downstairs to help her with her bags. Aunt Gbee was Mum's *little* sister and Jessame could soon hear her laughing and talking as she hurried up the stairs. Then she was in the kitchen, nearly filling it, and Grandma

and Grandpa were hugging her too.

Jessame watched them all from her bedroom doorway, and it seemed a long time before she heard Grandpa say, 'But where's Jessame Aduke? You haven't met Jessame Aduke yet.'

Then he fetched Jessame from the bedroom and Aunt Gbee said, 'Goodness gracious me, she's as pretty as a paw paw flower.'

And Jessame didn't know where to look. She wanted to look at Aunt Gbee but she knew it was rude to stare, and she was afraid that if she started to look, she wouldn't be able to stop. So she hid her face in Grandpa's shoulder and took little peeps, at little bits of her at a time — for Aunt Gbee was enormous! She had come all the way from *Sierra Leone* in Africa, Grandpa said, and he also said she was very tired, but she didn't look tired, not to Jessame. She looked very strong and very straight and very tall. She was so straight and so tall that Jessame wondered if she really was Grandma's daughter, because Grandma was small and round — and she was crying. Perhaps there had been a mistake? But Mum said Grandma was crying with happiness.

So there was Grandma, crying with happiness and dabbing her eyes and trying to fry onions all at the same time, because crispy fried onions and salt fish were Aunt Gbee's favourite breakfast. And there were Mum and Grandpa and Aunt Gbee all talking and laughing and saying, 'Do you remember?' over and over again. And there was Jessame feeling a bit hot. So she wriggled down from Grandpa and went to see Jacko.

Everybody had forgotten Jacko. He still had his cover on. Jessame took it off. Then she pressed her face against the bars of his cage and he pecked her nose fondly.

'Hello, Little Flower.'

'Hello, Jacko.'

'Hello, Little Flower.'

'Hello, Jacko. Has everybody forgotten you this morning?'

She gave him his breakfast of sunflower seeds and told him how glad she was to see him, how glad she was that he lived with them all the time, and how glad she was that he was small.

Then everybody else came into the sitting room for their breakfast. The table had been laid specially, with red serviettes, and Grandpa said, 'Eat heartily, daughter. Eat heartily, everybody.'

And Aunt Gbee piled her plate high with fish and crispy onions. Then she ate a mouthful very slowly and said, 'Mmmmm. It's seven long years since I tasted anything this good, Mummy, seven long years.'

Seven long years! Jessame felt a bit sorry for Aunt Gbee then. Fancy not tasting Grandma's cooking for seven long years! How had she grown so strong and straight?

Now, Jessame couldn't help staring a bit at Aunt Gbee — she was so tall even sitting down — but Aunt Gbee didn't mind. When she saw Jessame looking at her she just laughed and said she couldn't help looking at Jessame either, because she had never seen her before, except in photographs. She said she liked Jessame's red dressing-gown with ladybird buttons and she asked Jessame if she liked her costume. She meant her yellow dress with the wavy lines and the scarf to match, and Jessame said, 'I don't know, Aunt Gbee,' because she didn't. She wasn't sure about anything, and Aunt Gbee laughed again.

She didn't mind Jessame not knowing whether she liked her costume or not. Nor did she mind Jessame calling her Aunt G-bee. Grandpa had said that the G in Gbee was silent and that Jessame should say Aunt Bee, but Jessame had always said Aunt G-bee, ever since she'd started to read. Ever since she'd been a very little girl she'd always run to get the letters when the postman came, and she always knew Aunt Gbee's letters because the stamp had the seaside on it, with a very bright blue sky and a smart hotel. And on the back of the envelope it always said: 'From Gbee Williams.' Jessame had read it out to her mum and Mum hadn't explained about the silent letter G.

Jessame knew Aunt Gbee liked her. She'd brought her a dear little basket of flowers all the way from Sierra Leone. So Jessame wanted to like Aunt Gbee, in the same way that she liked Mum and Mark and Grandpa and Grandma. She *loved* them, but Aunt Gbee was *different*. She was so big. She was so bright and colourful that she seemed to Jessame to have stepped out of a picture book, and Jessame expected her to step back into it. But she didn't. She stayed, and lots of people came to see her.

Lots of people came to see her, and lots of them had their hair done – because Aunt Gbee was a hairdresser! This was very interesting. Jessame *was* sure about this. She loved watching Aunt Gbee do people's hair. Aunt Gbee did men's hair and ladies' hair – and Jessame's hair! She did it in all sorts of different styles, and she

asked Jessame which style she wanted. She did cane rows and corn rows — which were lots of little plaits — and dropped curls. Dropped curls were big curls that bounced when Jessame walked. They were her favourite. So she started to like Aunt Gbee quite a lot, and she thought she was going to like her even more. But then there was the birthday trouble.

Jessame's birthday was only three days away. She knew that because it was on the calendar in her bedroom, but no one mentioned it, even when Jessame mentioned it. It was very upsetting, and it seemed to Jessame that everybody had forgotten her birthday because they were so excited about seeing Aunt Gbee again.

But Jessame couldn't be sure. She couldn't be sure about Aunt Gbee and she couldn't be sure if everyone had really forgotten her birthday. The trouble was that for as long as she could remember, everyone at 56 Holly Bush House had always *pretended* to forget birthdays, but they didn't really, and you knew they didn't really, because secret things happened. For days before there was lots of coming back from the shop with secret packages. There was lots of going into the bedroom and closing the door and locking it — and lots of *rustling*.

That's what had happened before her birthday last year.

But this year she hadn't noticed anything like that. She thought that everyone had really forgotten. They had even forgotten her birthday cake, and she always had a very special birthday cake, even if she didn't have a party with friends, because she only had a party with friends sometimes. But always, a few days before her birthday, Mum would say, 'What's your favourite thing at the moment, Jessame?' And Jessame would tell her, and then Mum would make a birthday cake in the shape of her favourite thing. But she hadn't asked this year, even when her birthday was only one day away, and when Jessame said, 'I wonder what my birthday cake will be like this year,' — they were having tea at the time — it was as if no one had heard her.

When she said, 'I really loved the cake you made last year, which was like a fish tank with fishes in it,' Mum said, 'Well, I'd better make haste and get these dishes washed.' And she got up and left the table! It got worse and worse. When Mum came to kiss her goodnight, Jessame said, 'Are you going to work tomorrow, Mummy?' And Mum said "Yes," even though she always *always* had Jessame's birthday day off work. And in the morning, her birthday morning, no one said "Happy Birthday".

At school Mrs Pearce did say "Happy Birthday" and in assembly the whole school sang "Happy Birthday", but Jessame couldn't help feeling miserable. After assembly, Mrs Pearce said, 'What's the matter, Jessame? You don't look very happy,' and Jessame told her. Mrs Pearce was very kind. She said she was sure that Mum and Mark and Grandma and Grandpa Williams hadn't really forgotten. She said she was sure that they were pretending just as they had last year, and she was sure that when Jessame got home there would be a Big Surprise.

But there wasn't. Grandma Williams met her from school with Mark as usual, and took her home as usual. Mum wasn't there and nor was Grandpa — as usual. It seemed like an ordinary day — except for the strange smell.

The strange smell was coming from the kitchen. At first Jessame thought it was Aunt Gbee doing her hairdressing, because sometimes there were some very strange hairdressing smells, but this smell was different. It was a *nice* smell. In fact it was a *delicious* smell.

She said, 'What's that smell?'

And Grandma said, 'It's your top lip.' That was one of Grandma's expressions and she thought it was very funny. She laughed so much she wobbled and Jessame tried to go into the kitchen, but the door was locked.

So she went into the sitting room — and there was the table laid for a party! She knew it was, because everything was covered with a big white cloth, the same as last year. And there were interesting lumps underneath and serviettes and party poppers peeping out, the same as last year. And when she lifted a corner of the big white cloth she came face to face with an alligator! That wasn't the same as last year. The alligator was made out of a cucumber! And there were giraffes made of sausages and sandwiches shaped like elephants. There was a whole zoo under that table cloth!

Jessame counted the plates. There were eleven.

'Who's coming? Who's coming?'

Grandma wouldn't tell her.

'Go and get your party frock on, Jessame. They'll be here any minute now.'

As Jessame passed the kitchen on the way to her bedroom the delicious sweet smell smelt even more delicious. It was a sweet spicy smell. She

tried the door handle but it still wouldn't move.
  'Who's in there?'
Nobody answered.
  'Mum?
Grandpa?

Aunt Gbee?'

Still nobody answered.

'Get along with you. Make haste now.' Grandma hurried her into the bedroom and there was her lacy blue party dress on the bed and so were her shiny black patent leather shoes. Grandma helped her into the dress and just as Jessame was sticking her head out of the top she heard Jason's voice - and Jamila's and the voices of Vicki and Penny from the other end of the verandah. They didn't go to Jessame's school.

Jessame rushed into the sitting room and all four friends gave her presents. And then Mum and Grandpa came home early from work and they gave her presents. And Mum showed her the birthday cake hidden in the sideboard; it was a parrot cake – like Jacko! And then there was Uncle Sharp home from sea! He said he had a present for her at the bottom of his kitbag.

What a lot of secrets had been kept. What a lot of people. Jessame counted. Ten. One was missing. Who was it?

Then the kitchen door opened and the delicious smell of sweetness burst out, followed by Aunt Gbee wearing her yellow dress with wavy lines.

She was waving a wooden spoon.

'What is it? What is that delicious smell?'
Everybody was asking.

'Come and see,' said Aunt Gbee. 'The Birthday Girl first. Come on, Jessame.'

Jessame followed Aunt Gbee into the kitchen. Jamila and Jason and Vicki and Penny followed Jessame. Then they all stood in a line behind her as she stepped up to the stove. The delicious smell was growing more delicious by the second.

It was coming from a heavy pan inside which was a golden liquid.

'What is it? What is it?'

Aunt Gbee handed Jessame the wooden spoon.

'Stir, stir and you will see,
It needs five good stirs to make _____ .'

She didn't finish the rhyme but Jessame stirred the golden liquid which was bubbling in the pan, with little bubbles round the edge and big bubbles in the middle. Then Jason stirred, then Jamila, then Vicki, then Penny.

'That's right. *Five good stirs*,' said Aunt Gbee when all five children had had a go.

'To make what?' said Jessame.

Aunt Gbee laughed. 'Can't you guess, Jess?'

'No.'

'Well, look all around you.'

'Look,' said Aunt Gbee, picking up a tray. 'Here's some that I made earlier.'

She sounded just like the cooks on the telly

as she popped a piece of the sticky deliciousness into Jessame's mouth.

And then Jessame knew what was on Aunt Gbee's tray, and what was in the pan, and what was on plates and dishes and trays and saucers all over the kitchen.

'Stir, stir and you will see,

It takes five good stirs to make TOFFEE!'

It was the most wonderful toffee she had ever tasted, a million trillion times more delicious than the toffee she had tasted from shops. This toffee tasted of sweetness and sunny days and spicy warmth. It tasted of hot beaches and jugs of cream, of vanilla and caramel. It was smooth and sticky and chewy and licky, and it stayed in the mouth for just the right length of time before it melted into nothingness – and then there was *more*!

'But not yet,' said Aunt Gbee.

First they had to play Birthday games.

Then they had to eat the Birthday tea.

And then it would be Birthday Toffee Time! They could all eat as much as they liked and if there was any left they could all have a bag full to take home.

'But what about me?' said Jessame. 'I *am* at home.'

Then Aunt Gbee lifted the big heavy pan from off the stove and poured the golden liquid into another tray. 'This,' she said, 'is for later. This is Family Birthday Toffee for when everyone else has gone home.'

It was the best birthday Jessame had ever had. The games were really exciting and the zoo tea was scrumptious, but the best thing about the birthday was the Birthday Toffee. Everybody thought so. Aunt Gbee said she thought it was the Muscovado sugar which made it so special, but Jessame said she was *sure* it was Aunt Gbee.